The Great Malvern Paradox

GORDON LOCKHART

To Carol.

CONTENTS

ACKNOWLEDGMENTS

Carol, who thought (rightly) that my first draft read like a school essay, and corrected numerous grammatical mistakes. The stories themselves were inspired by the University of Edinburgh's excellent Massive Open Online Course (MOOC) on "Introduction to Philosophy".

The Experimental Philosophy Unit

Jim woke up and blinked at precisely the same time as the other 36 in the ward. Looking round, he found himself near the end of a poorly-lit, cavernous ward, seemingly populated by male patients, all peering into the gloom just as he was. He had been dozing on a bench in his favourite courtyard surrounded by some of Edinburgh's finest old tenements when suddenly an enormous black insect had flown up out of nowhere and stung him on the face – "What the !! ......" and then oblivion. Touching his face now, he felt no marks or pain. "So far so good", he thought. He even felt hungry.

"Your attention please, gentlemen!" This from a bright but strangely flustered young lady who had entered unsteadily through the door beside Jim's bed and was doing her best to address them. She wore an odd but expensive looking tunic and a narrow, draped skirt. It was wide at the hips but so narrow at the ankle she had difficulty in walking. "There is no need to panic!" she exclaimed as if there really were some reason for alarm. Jim smiled at the spectacle and subdued laughter rose from the other beds. A little nonplussed she continued, "Everything you need is here. You'll find clothes under the bed. There's a washroom over there, buffet and bar next door – just help yourself – any questions?" Then she turned on her heel and headed back to the door. As she passed Jim he noticed the letters "EPU" emblazoned on her sleeve and called out, "Nurse! What does EPU stand for?" "I'm not a nurse Jim29 – the name's Sue", she replied and hobbled away as quickly as her skirt would allow. "Why's she wearing my grandmother's best clothes? " said a voice beside him. Peering at bed 28 next to his own, he made out a stocky, middle-aged man of about the same age and build as himself. "Dunno – thought she was a nurse – yeah, reminds me of my grandmother's Sunday best too."

chortled Jim29. "The name's Jim28 by the way" said the man, smiling as he stuck out his hand. "Gent beside me's another Jim – Jim27 I call him – coincidence eh?" Jim29 grasped the outstretched hand. "Sure is!" said another voice from bed 30, "Jim30 here too!"

The four Jims put on the old fashioned clothes they found under their beds, but left the cloth caps. They were all hungry so they took some sandwiches from the buffet into the bar and washed them down with the free beer. The others from the ward had had the same idea and soon all 37 were in the bar discussing their predicament – but with ever-increasing anxiety. All 37 had the same first name and closely resembled each other – right down to the beginnings of 37 beer paunches. Jim29 disliked exchanging surnames or much personal information with strangers and the other Jims seemed to share his aversion but what they found really weird was that they had all suffered the same type of accident. "Pesky insects carrying some horrible infection maybe" said Jim29. Jim28 agreed and thought they'd been dumped into a secret isolation ward somewhere and they had better find out who was in charge. There were some big questions to put to Sue in the morning.

But what happened in the morning was completely unexpected. Jims 28 and 29 were having breakfast together. Jim28, still determined to find someone in charge, raised his hand, pointed a finger then suddenly froze – motionless. Jim29 followed the gaze of Jim28's unblinking eyes but saw nothing unusual, just the other Jims chatting or silently munching their breakfasts. "What is it Jim?" The seconds passed but Jim28 neither spoke nor moved, his hand and finger suspended stiffly in mid-air, his mouth fixed half open in silent protestation. Jim29 was thoroughly alarmed by now but before he could act Sue tottered out of a side door carrying a large white sheet that she threw over Jim28's inert body. Effortlessly scooping him up from his chair she marched off with him under one arm as if he was a tailor's dummy. "What happened there? Was that Sue?", asked Jim30 anxiously from the next table. Momentarily delayed when Jim28's rigid index finger caught on the door handle, Sue managed to lock the door behind her before the two Jims could catch her up. They banged on the door and eventually she emerged, embarrassed. "Look guys, I'm sorry. It was my fault. Please don't say anything. Jim28 took ill but he'll be OK. I can't really tell you any more but there's no need to panic". She shuffled awkwardly as a large crowd of Jims began to gather round. "You'd better tell us more Sue!", retorted Jim29 angrily. "For a start, where are we and what's going on here?" "Yeah!" sang the crowd in unison as they demanded to know where Jim28 had gone. "Sorry gentlemen!", said Sue as she turned to go.

Now Jim had never laid a finger on anyone before – certainly not a lady. He was a paragon of virtue in that respect, drunk or sober, but he lost it now. Sticking out a foot like a demented footballer he brought Sue down in a flurry of tunic and skirt. She lay on the floor in some distress until a couple of the other Jims helped her up. "Why did you do that Jim29?" she wailed. "I'm sorry Sue, but I had no choice. It was the right thing to do. We're stuck here with no explanations. You're not leaving until you've told us what's going on." Sue recovered and astonished them all by smiling delightedly. "It was the right thing to do." she repeated. "Note the subject's unemotional demeanour indicative of objective moral opinion. This is unarguably a relativistic moral situation and furthermore a case of ...", she gabbled on. "Stop it!" shouted Jim29. "We want some answers – now!" Startled, she retorted, "I'm only taking notes for the experiment...... oh gee!" She tailed off …

Crestfallen once more, she told them that working for the Experimental Philosophy Unit was no easy option and that mistakes did happen. She'd fluffed the 'copy and paste' and now there were 37 Jims – 37 of them, guinea pigs in a thought experiment where there ought to have been just one. "You mean we're … clones?" interrupted Jim29. Sure enough, examining each other's features confirmed just that – down to the least pimple and hair follicle. "But what happened to Jim28?" asked another Jim. "I had to take him away", explained Sue. "I thought I'd be in trouble. You're not very heavy when your module's suspended – defaults to a surface representation in a light wire frame so I just took him away. You can't have your reality shattered by people suddenly vanishing into thin air now can you? Anyway, the experiment's ruined now that you know everything and I'll be in trouble for wasting resources again. And these stupid clothes are just killing me! I can't see why you like them!" The Jims looked at each other blankly. Sue continued, "I thought you'd feel more at home but you all just laughed! Best 1914 fashions too – I checked it all out with the Edinburgh store!" Jim29 told her gently that this was in fact 2014. "Oh No! ..I've never been any good with numbers since that Jamie from Epistemology told me they don't exist – and anyway", she pouted, "19's right next door to 20, isn't it? – it's an easy enough mistake to make. My project's on early 20th century working class moral relativism – now it's ruined! How can I probe the moral scruples of a 1914 working class man when I'm lumbered with 37 cloned Jims from the wrong century? And she started to cry.

Jim29 took a very long, deep breath. "So we're nothing but robots or zombies or something then?" "No no, that's not it, of course you're not" she sobbed, you're manifestations – but I can't expect you to understand that!" Jim pinched himself and duly winced. Was he dreaming? "No you're not dreaming. You're all sentient beings just like me." she said, having regained some composure. "Well then, if your experiment is off can't we all just go home now?" asked Jim29 but Jim17 wanted to know how this could happen. The thought of 37 Jims returning to the same home was not attractive. There would be no end of trouble with wives and families. Heated arguments broke out among the Jims about who would get home and several punches were thrown. "I'll see to it gentlemen!" soothed Sue anxiously. "I did some really smart identity switching during a Brain in a Vat experiment after someone knocked a vat over – well, OK, it was me but I managed to convince the brain he was drunk at the time. So we patched him up and plugged him into a new vat before he sobered up. He lived happily for years after without getting any fancy sceptical ideas about reality!"

Before the Jims could absorb any of this, Jim17 suddenly froze and keeled over. "No problem at all" shrieked Sue trying to make herself heard above the clamour. "You've killed him you ..." shouted Jim32, only to freeze and topple over himself. The other 35 Jims stepped back, wondering in alarm who would be next. "They're not killed. I've only suspended their modules" explained Sue, exasperated. Sure enough Jim17 promptly picked himself up from the floor, a little shaken but all in one piece. "What happened?", he spluttered. "I'm standing up talking and then I'm on the floor, without falling, fainting or anything?". "I just saved your status and then re-activated you to show the others I'm not a murderer" said Sue proudly but she wouldn't resurrect Jim32. "Miracles don't come cheap" she beamed. "I can't turn water into wine every day but there's no problem. Jim32 goes home but with no memory at all of this place. The few hours he spent here with us won't be mourned by anyone, will they? I'll fix it for you all to lose your memories of here even if I use the very last of my resource allowance to do it!" Her brow furrowed in wrapt contemplation.

Jim furiously swiped at his face and the insect buzzed away into the distance. There was no pain or even the presence of sting marks. It seemed inconceivable to him that dreaming about the ward and all the other Jims could have happened between the insect coming and now – but the mind does play tricks. He was just about to stand up and leave when he spotted a lady in fancy dress hobbling towards him from the other side of the courtyard. As she approached, the tunic and the narrow, draped skirt, assumed a terrible familiarity.

Sue stopped beside him and announced in a haughty voice, "Please excuse me kind Sir. Do you have the time of day?" Jim was flabbergasted. "Sue! What on earth are you doing here?" Now Sue was flabbergasted. Dropping the haughty tone, she flopped down beside him with some difficulty. "I was just testing to see if you remembered anything but that really is odd. All your memories of the ward should have gone by now! Silly me! My resource allowance is gone so I'm afraid you'll just have to live with it. But everything else will be OK – just go home as usual and relax." Jim sighed with undisguised relief but he still wanted to know what had happened to him and why he seemed to be wearing the same clothes he'd had on in the ward, plus that cloth cap. "For a start, what's the Experimental Philosophy Unit all about?" She seemed quite willing to tell him.

"Well, we did a lot of these old thought experiments. You know the sort of thing. If you really were a brain in a vat could you ever know it? Plato's Caves, Evil Demons, Deities – you name it, we've got them all, raring to go but it's not always been plain sailing. It took scores of shepherds and fake sheep and we never solved the Justified True Belief thing. We had a great run of Fat Man experiments though. Somebody decides whether or not to save the lives of six people in a runaway trolley on a railway line by pushing a fat man off a railway bridge to his death – right in front of the trolley." Jim was horrified. "I don't believe it! You'd kill fat men –

just as an experiment?" She looked puzzled. "Of course you could. It's either him or six die! That's the whole point – it's a moral dilemma but most people let the six die anyway and we wanted to know why. Mind you, one time it all went horribly wrong with a group of pacifists. Not one of them would push the fat man off the bridge and he got so cross he jumped off the bridge by himself and missed the runaway trolley altogether. Everyone got killed and I had to fiddle the statistics!" Jim had had enough. "That's ghastly!", he spluttered. "If any of this is true then it's criminal and if it's not, you're badly in need of help!" Sue paused to think, "Good logic Jim", she said sternly, "But truth can be relative, compossible as we say in the trade. Look, your moral indignation is all well and good in the right place but the Fat Man is one of our best zombies and loves being pushed off bridges. I really didn't mean to annoy him but I thought the pacifists were pastors – an easy enough mistake and I did spend the rest of the afternoon pushing him off the bridge myself to make it up to him."

At this point Jim was having serious doubts about Sue's sanity and was beginning to question his own when he noticed for the first time a couple of fine gas lamps on the wall opposite. Then, glancing up he became aware of a trio of

chattering ladies entering the
courtyard followed by a small boy
chasing a hoop – all fashionably
dressed in the same style as Sue.
A couple of working class men
sauntered by wearing cloth caps
and old clothes – just like his …..
He looked at Sue …."Don't panic!",
she whimpered.

Grandfathers' Paradox

A pint o' heavy an' a whisky
chaser, Ewan!" said the tall, quite
handsome young man in his cloth
cap and working clothes. He
collected his drinks, looked
around until he spotted an empty
seat and fought his way through
the heaving crowd to Jim and
Sue's table. Jim grimaced as the
man splashed down his drinks.
Startled, Sue looked up.

"Sorry hen! Dinnae mind me."

smiled the man and added hesitatingly, "The name's Tam." "I'm Sue and this is my brother Jim – pleased to meet you!", said Sue brightly as she helped herself to the liquorice drops Tam offered from a large poke.

Trapped in 1914 Edinburgh in what might or might not be a bad dream was not at all to Jim's liking and neither was being persuaded by Sue into the 'Deacon Brodie' pub posing as her brother. She was determined to improve her standing with the Experimental Philosophy Unit (EPU) and Jim understood this well enough to know that his returning to 2014 depended on her success and his co-operation.

Deacon Brodie's Tavern – Edinburgh 2005 (Image by Stephen Curtin on Flickr)

"Whit's yer poison then" queried Tam looking at their empty glasses.

Jim shot Sue a warning glance but she smiled broadly at Tam.

"Oh – a pint of heavy please – and a lemonade for my brother!"

Tam, expecting a dusty reply, chuckled at what he took to be a joke. When he was back he plonked the beer down in front of Jim who hurriedly took a sip before Sue could stop him. Tam grinned at her mischievously.

"I couldnae get a lady's glass for the beer but there's a dash o' vodka in yer lemonade!"

"Cheers!", said Sue. "Doon the hatch" said Tam.

Jim sipped his beer morosely

while Sue and Tam cheerfully conversed. Sue claimed to be a writer from London researching her new book on 'Working Men of the North' and eager to interview Tam. She handed him a crisp new pound note.

"Something on account – and oh! … I've finished my lemonade!" Tam took the hint and went off to buy more drinks.

"Jim, I really am sorry that my project on early 20th century working class moral relativism got you stuck back in 1914 but here we are and we might as well make the best of it. Tam could be an ideal subject with a strong moral sense. I could finish off my project here and the EPU would be so

pleased I'd probably get all the resources I need to spirit you back to 2014. Anyway, I really like Tam. Let's see what I can do."
So when Tam returned she opened a notebook and began to interrogate him about his early life. Feeling a little left out, Jim bought a copy of 'The War Cry' from a Salvation army seller doing the pub rounds and settled down to read.

Tam spotted the paper's title. "Aye, I hope it disnae cam to war. My wee brither, Alan, he's wantin' to jine the Scot's Guards; only 16 an he'll lie aboot his age if he can!" Jim looked up. "Same name as my granduncle! He joined the Scot's Guards too but sadly he was ....

HEY!"

Sue, waving her notebook at an imaginary fly, knocked his beer over.

"Sorry Jim!", she exclaimed loudly, "Go get him another Tam!"

Tam went off with another pound note while Sue glared at Jim.

"Don't make that sort of remark in front of Tam!".

Jim protested that it really was quite a coincidence about Tam's brother and his granduncle.

"Hmm – maybe less of a coincidence than you think. Maybe Alan could be your granduncle in 2014 but do remember where you are in time!"

Jim dropped his paper and stared at Sue. Then another thought struck him.

"Grandfather's name was Thomas but he was always called…"
Before Sue could reply Tam was back with the drinks.

Conversation turned to the chances of war breaking out. Tam was certain war would be averted but Sue was more pessimistic and summarised the confused state of 1914 international politics with considerable accuracy. Tam was very impressed.

"Yer a clever wee lassie, I've nae doot, but tak it fay me – it cannae happen. Things dinnae happen by chance."

"Oh but they do, they do!" Sue gulped down the rest of her drink, "And I'll show you how!"

Jim looked on in some alarm while Tam went off with yet another note for more drinks. Sue, scrabbling under the table, emerged with handfuls of debris from the floor and proceeded to build a large circular pyramid of sawdust, fag ends and bottle tops on the table top. Tam, back with the drinks, watched with amusement as Sue stood up to demonstrate.

"The pyramid is the universe – life, everything we know", she announced grandly, attracting the attention of several nearby drinkers.

"With careful management things evolve gradually – on they go in a regular way and everyone's happy.

But see how a tiny change can bring about terrible cataclysmic changes, changing eveything for ever!"

Nudging the tip of the pyramid she caused rivulets of sawdust to cascade and spread downwards, sticking on some obstacles and carrying away others in the flow. She paused only to finish the rest of her drink.

"A cascade of cause and effect! A small chance disturbance of grains near the top dislodges more further down and then others even further down in a chain reaction, but not necessarily so and very unpredictably."

Becoming bored the crowd began to dwindle.

"Look, here!" and she gestured dramatically at a stopped rivulet. "Aye, stopped – by a fag end." countered Tam in mock solemnity and the remaining onlookers tittered. Sue glared at him. "A tiny trivial change MIGHT cause major changes or it might not; a critical uncertainty as we say in the EPU. World political systems are on a knife edge at this time. Tam's brother wants to join the army and he's only 16! I know he'll be sent to an early death along with thousands of others!..."

She talked at length about the ravages of war, tears welling in her eyes and Jim could see they were genuine. How much vodka had Tam put in her drinks? But Tam was standing open-mouthed at the front of the now swelling crowd, lost in admiration. "Nonsense! Let the youmg lad join for king and country!" someone heckled. There was some supportive cheering, some dissension and then several arguments broke out. A shout of "Workers of the world unite!" followed and for no obvious reason two scruffy-looking youths at the front yelled, "Up the EPU!" and started to bellow the 'Red Flag'. A punch was thrown somewhere followed by several others and soon the whole pub was brawling. Just then the police burst in.

The steam train huffed and puffed its way slowly out of Waverley Station in a cloud of dirty smoke. Jim sighed. Running off to London just to escape a pub brawl seemed over-reacting. The two scruffy youths had helped Jim, Sue and Tam evade the police and head for the station. Sue, in what Jim took to be drunken magnanimity, had bought them all return tickets. This had followed a mysterious chat with an old man she found on the platform who eagerly accepted a handful of her pound notes.

"Change of plan! – Found a Grandfather!" she had hissed in Jim's ear as he helped her onto the train.

Settled in their compartment, the two youths, introduced themselves as Adam and Vojtech.

Both insisted they were on their way to London for an urgent meeting anyway and Tam was keen to continue his interview with Sue and benefit further from her generosity. Adam explained that Ewan the barman had called the police because someone had been passing forged pound notes with identical serial numbers. Startled, Sue fished out a small cigarette rolling machine from her handbag. At the touch of a button a pristine pound note glided out from between the rollers, then another and another.

"All absolutely identical!", she said with feeling. "But I forgot the numbers had to be different!"

Adam and Vojtech looked at her

with a new respect.

"A brilliant orator and now an expert forger!" gasped Adam.

Vojtech asked what EPU stood for.

"Experimental Philosophy Unit but I can't tell you more...", retorted Sue truthfully.

"Ahhh, clever!" Vojtech touched his nose and smiled knowingly.

"You are right to hide – our mission hidden too." Adam interjected,

"Always happy to assist comrades in need. The revolution – a critical certainty! Ha! Ha! – loved the demo."

"We deliver stuff to blackened handle and..." muttered Vojtec darkly but Adam blew his nose noisily and the rest was inaudible.

GORDON LOCKHART

Jim wondered if Tam would be missed at home but his Mam was used to him being away. He was more worried about the girl he was courting.

"Christine's a braw lassie but whit a temper! 'Thomas MacPherson!', she'll say, 'WHAT have ye been up tae?' I wouldnae dare cross her! Today she's aff to see her mither on the next train but ....." but Jim MacPherson was not listening. Certainty dawned. Tam is / was / would be his grandfather because his grandmother's name happened to be – Christine.

When they saw two railway policeman boarding the train at the next station Tam and the two youths scuttled off to find the bufffet carriage leaving Jim and Sue alone in the compartment.

Sue beamed.

"It's okay Jim. I've got it all worked out now. Nobody's ever properly tackled the Grandfather Paradox before you know."

Before Jim could make anything of that a large railway policeman appeared at the door and asked politely to see any pound notes they were carrying. Jim held his breath as Sue nonchalantly handed him several from her purse.

"Sorry to bother you Madam. Somebody passed off some duds at Waverley but these are fine!" and off he went.

"How did you do that?" asked Jim.

Sue shrugged. She had no idea how notes were numbered in 1914 so she just had her machine do random numbers.

Jim had many more questions but then Tam returned demanding to know who Sue really was. Sue, by now almost sober, held to her story about being a writer and placated him with two randomly numbered pound notes on account of his unfinished interview. Tam was motivated to pass round more liquorice drops but he was convinced the youths were up to no good. Maybe they ought to look inside the cloth bag Vojtech's had left on his seat? They did. The bag was surprisingly heavy with the contents wrapped in several layers of dirty linen like a set of China dolls. They were astonished to find a large pistol along with a small bottle labelled 'Not to be Taken'. Tam examined the pistol.

"Pop was a poacher!" he winked, expertly opening up the pistol and fingering the mechanism until he discovered it was loaded. When they heard the two youths noisily returning down the corridor, Tam pushed everything back into the bag and Sue restarted the interview.

Now Jim was unfamiliar with the philosophy of time travel but the grandfather paradox was very well-known. Go back in time and kill your own grandfather. Would you cease to exist – or what? Well here he was back in time with his grandfather in close proximity to a loaded gun. Could Sue be intent on experimental verification of the paradox?

A sudden and furious commotion in the corridor; just as Tam stood up a short woman in a headscarf burst in lunging at him with a cloth bag.

"Hey!", yelled Tam, collapsing beside Sue. "Cut that oot!"

"So this is the trollop yer aff wi! So help me, I'll niver speak to ye again!"

But she did and throwing her bag accurately at his head she screamed, "TAK THAT, ye bastard! Ye'll be sorry by the time I'm finished wi ye!"

She stormed off, stopping only to scoop up the bag on the way out.

Tam rubbed his head sadly.

"Ah thought Chris wis on the next train!"

Sue went after Christine to try to explain. Tam, less disconsolate about Christine than he might have been, wanted to talk to Jim in private. They went out into the corridor as Adam and Vojtech began bellowing 'The Red Flag' again.

Tam was serious. "Yer sister's a bonnie wee lassie, clever tae – for a wummin that is. Noo that Chris's finished wi me ah think I'd like tae walk oot wi Sue. I ken she likes me and I hope ye dinnae mind."

Jim said nothing which Tam took for tacit agreement but Jim was greatly troubled by the thought of Sue as an alternative grandmother. Would he simply cease to exist if his grandmother was not Christine? On the other hand if that was the case why was he even here now? Maybe there was hope but ceasing to exist might mean an untimely death for him here but if it was all a dream anyway .....

The train stopped at a station to pick up more passengers and several piles of luggage and mailbags. Peering out into the corridor Adam saw the large railway policeman striding towards their compartment. He rushed out

the door and slunk down the
corridor in the opposite direction.
Vojtech grabbed the cloth bag.
"Now lads that's quite enough
song for now.." began the
policeman sternly from the
compartment door.

"Off back!" shouted Vojtech, "I
have gun!"

The policeman backed away
nervously as Vojtech opened the
bag. A small metal comb jangled
onto the floor followed by a tube of
lipstick, a red toothbrush and
several tissues. The policeman
grinned and rapidly grabbed and
handcuffed the astonished
Vojtech.

"Oldest trick in the book – eh?",
chuckled the policeman.

"You're in for it pal!" and he marched Vojtech off the train.

No other cloth bag could be found so they concluded that Christine must have taken Vojtech's bag. The implications were not lost on Tam as he hurriedly packed Christine's personal belongings back into her bag. A minute later the sound of pounding feet echoed down the corridor. Adam ran by in distress shouting at them as he passed. "Look out! She's really mad and she's got a ...!"
Looking out into the corridor Jim and Tam spotted a distant but rapidly approaching Christine waving something above her head and shouting, "Tam! Tam!"

GORDON LOCKHART

Jim and Tam, with different but compelling fears of impending non-existence both closed their eyes as Christine burst into the compartment throwing herself at Tam who begged for mercy. He felt her swiping the side of his face with something.

"Hey! Dinnae be funny!", she said excitedly,"Look whit I've got!"

Jim slowly opened his eyes to see Christine brandishing a large roll of pound notes. When Christine realised that Tam had her bag she smothered him with hugs and kisses and hoped he'd seen off that thief Adam with more than a black eye.

"And noo we can afford to get marriet!", she announced to the world and dragged Tam off to visit her mother.

Jim had just about convinced himself that these events were definitely the stuff of dreams when Sue returned with a perfectly rational explanation. She had hurried after Christine who had locked herself in the loo. Shouting through the door, Sue told her that Tam had acted honourably in agreeing to be interviewed for her book. Christine was only fully convinced when Sue, now desperate, persuaded her that Tam would put his interview fee towards his future with Christine. As they walked back along the corridor, she gave Christine a substantial roll of pound notes on account. About to put away the money, Christine realised she had left her bag in the loo and rushed back just in time to see Adam running off with it. So off she went after him in a fury, waving the money roll and shouting for Tam.

Sue laughed at Jim's account of what had happened.
"So all's well that ends well but you still look worried Jim?"
Jim tried to explain that ceasing to exist if something had happened to his grandfather-to-be was more than worrisome. Sue laughed again.
"Existentialist angst, eh? That's not how it works Jim. If Tam died now you'd never meet your Dad or your young self if you stayed on

here. A critical uncertainty for you and your family for sure but probably not for the rest of the world. Mind you, it would be more difficult for me to get you back to your proper timeline in 2014. On the other hand, if you stayed on here without Tam meeting an early demise you could have some really strange meet-ups with your relatives and friends to be. Don't worry though, if you or they couldn't remember anything about it in 2014 then it probably didn't happen."

She looked round making sure that they would stay alone.

"Look Jim, you know that a certain Gavrilo Princip will assassinate an Archduke in

Sarajevo in a couple of days time and trigger off the first world war? Now if you went off right now and murdered Princip before he even had the chance to get near the poor Archduke, that really would be a disaster for both of us unless something else happened to start the war."

She decided to confide in Jim.

"You probably think that I'm very wise and knowledgeable Jim."

Jim thought no such thing and Sue continued.

"I'm only a very junior member of the EPU and I was in very big trouble when my copy and paste went wrong and I cloned 37 identical Jims from the wrong century."

Jim did remember.

"But you must admit that I got you back to your own timeline – a 100 year error is not bad in over 2000!"

Jim sighed.

"All the same, I've never studied your timeline without a first world war and a radical divergence could be interesting if it happened – a monumental change in world history! But if it did, I'd have absolutely no idea how to get you back, even if I had the resources and you'd be stuck here for ever! Not to worry, it's certainly a critical uncertainty for the world but we've absolutely no connections with Princip and he's probably gearing up at this very moment to do his dastardly deed. ..... Hold on!", and she paused "Something's coming through now from that grandfather I left at Waverley Station......"

She muttered silently to herself in a few moments of concentration.
"Good news Jim! I HAVE verified the Grandfather Paradox!"
Jim looked blank.
"Tam didn't know it but I planted a deadly accurate chronometer on him when he boarded the train and now he's a few femtoseconds younger than that grandfather I paid to stay on the platform at Waverly!"
Jim stared at her in disbelief.
"That's not the Grandfather

Paradox!"

"Of course it is! Maybe you're more familiar with the original formulation" she said condescendingly.

"Two grandfathers – one makes a journey into space in a high-speed rocket but when he comes back he finds the grandfather who stayed on Earth has aged more. Great experiment but my way of doing it is far more straightforward!"

"That's not the Grandfather Paradox! That's the Twin Paradox – it's done with twins!"

"Nonsense!" She began to look a little defensive. "It's done with grandfathers!"

Jim forgot it was 1914.

"You only need to look at

Wikipedia!"

"Oh!" she said, worried. "I'm looking …. you can't always trust Wikipedia." but she knew she was clutching at straws.

"Let's go home now" she said, crestfallen.

A few days later Ewan scrutinised Jim's pound note carefully in the 'Deacon Brodie'.

"One for yourself?" Jim asked the barman nervously.

"No problems there now.", smiled Sue when Jim returned with the drinks.

She was very cheerful and had been in touch with the EPU. To her great surprise, her twins experiment, now correctly renamed, had gone down extremely well with the top brass. Damaging criticism about wasting resources on unscientific experiments had been countered by pointing to Sue's groundbreaking work on relativistic physics! Now she had every hope for extra resources and was sure Jim would get home, "in no time at all! – Ha! Ha!" she chuckled in an attempt at humour. Jim smiled with relief. "So all's really well that ends well!" he concluded.

A loud conversation was going on a few tables away.

"Aye, efter shootin the Archduke this Princip boy fae the Black Hand – tried to kill himsel but the poison didnae work. Then he tried tae droon himsel but the river wis only 4 inches deep – whit a loser!"

"What did I tell you?" Sue whispered quietly. "I don't like to celebrate a killing but this was a very critical uncertainty – it had to happen for us!"

They clinked their glasses together. A woman continued the conversation at the other table.

"Whit a cheek!" she chortled heartily.

Unaccountably, she and her friends burst into laughter

stomping their feet noisely on the floor. Sue and Jim listened intently.

"Aye, if the pistol had been true the Archduke wid have mair than a grazed cheek!"

Jim and Sue stared at each other aghast.

Then Tam entered the pub and came over looking very serious.

"Did ye no hear aboot the Archduke? An that Adam and Vojtec? I kent they wis up to nae guid – they were takin that pistol tae the Black Hand! – a bunch o' assassins!"

Tam looked round furtively and hissed, "I should hae taen oot the bullets! At least ah filled his wee suicide bottle wi liquorice drops!"

Tam showed them the morning newspaper. The headline, 'Failed Assassination Attempt Could Herald World Peace' was followed by an article on how the attempted assassination had brought shocked world leaders to their senses at last. Recognising the dangers of the current complex system of political alliances they had hastily convened a conference to guarantee world peace and stability. An international body, a 'Club of Nations' was now under serious consideration!

Sue turned white.
"I telt ye there wudnae be war, wummin", said Tam kindly.
"Don't panic!", she said quietly to Jim and began to cry.

Taken aback, Tam threw his arms round Sue and kissed her – she did not resist. Just then Christine came in.

THE GREAT MALVERN PARADOX

The Water Cure

Maybe it was the beer but Jim was quite relaxed given the alarming circumstances. Here he was in an Edinburgh pub, dreaming or not, trapped a hundred years in the past with crazy Sue from something called the Experimental Philosophical Unit (EPU) who at this very moment was kissing his grandfather-to-be. The global predicament was crazy too. World War 1 had not started on cue and if that was not enough, Christine, his grandmother-to-be, was heading right now for his grandfather-to-be, with a broken bottle in her hand and murder in her eye.

"Now clear the way, **PLEASE !!**" A short balding man in a doctor's white coat and a stethoscope hanging ostentatiously from his neck had entered the pub by a side entrance. Shoving his way through a crowd of drinkers to Jim's table, he managed to arrive just before the irate Christine angrily brandishing her broken bottle.

"Very well done Tam!", exclaimed the doctor loudly, shaking Tam vigorously by the shoulder. "Couldnae do better mysel! I do believe the lassie's breathin' fine noo but I'd better tak her tae hospital for a check up."

Tam, taken by surprise,
promptly released Sue while the
doctor turned to Christine, now
stopped in her tracks.

"Aye, he saved this poor lassie's
life! Did ye learn the kiss o' life at
yer first aid class Tam?"

Here he poked a startled Tam.

"Aye!", spluttered Tam, eager for
any way out.

Christine's jaw dropped as did the
broken bottle and she ran over to
embrace Tam.

"Oh Tam! – I'm sorry Tam – oh my
hero!"

Colliding heavily with Tam she
grabbed him so tightly that he lost
his balance and they both fell on
the floor.

Jim, Sue and the doctor took

the opportunity to beat a hasty exit through the side door. The doctor, who said his name was Simon, led them through a network of dark alleyways climbing upwards towards the castle until they reached a doorway marked, 'Camera Obscura'. Simon entered, quickly paid the doorman and ushered them all up a dark spiral staircase. He pushed open the door at the very top and they entered a small darkened room. Simon managed to jam the door closed behind them.

"It's only Simon from the EPU", Sue hissed in Jim's ear. "... and I don't like him!"
Jim thought this a

little ungracious considering her
escape from Christine's vengeance
but Simon had already launched
into a lecture on the Camera
Obscura.
"This device, installed here in
1853, projects a panoramic view of
the city below onto the flat
horizontal surface you see before
you. A Camera Obscura consists
of a box or room with a small hole
allowing light from an external
source to pass through and project
an image of an external scene
and...."

Someone was trying the door
from the outside.
"Of course nobody here knows it
but all Obscura rooms are
entangled right across the globe,

so we of the EPU can conveniently
hop around just about anywhere
in space and time. 'Spooky action
at a distance' as Einstein would
say or will say – ha! ha! – or maybe
not, I forgot we're on the wrong
timeline now. I think he gave up
physics on this one and went into
pharmaceuticals."
The knocking at the door became
louder but Simon continued.
"Don't worry Jim. This Obscura
room exists in your 2014 so I'll
just make a few adjustments and
drop you off there before
continuing with my own important
mission."
Jim could hardly believe his luck
as Simon closed his eyes and
raised both arms dramatically.

"Just a minute while I set up a control panel or we'll just end up wherever the last user went." Gradually the panoramic image before them became lost in a thickening, spherically-shaped cloud of pink smoke. A series of rods and dials of various sizes and colours began to protrude from it at odd angles.

"This is ludicrous. He's just showing off!", said Sue none too quietly.

She backed away from the smoke coughing loudly.

Now the knocking at the door was incessant.

"Open up yous in there!" somebody shouted, "Come on noo!"

Simon dropped his arms in exasperation and went off to remonstrate with those outside the door.

"Let's open a window" said Sue. She pulled up a blind covering a small window and pushed it wide open.

"That's better!", she cried as a wisp of pink smoke lazily turned towards the window and darted outside.The wisp was followed more rapidly by another and yet another until the entire cloud, replete with levers and dials had moved towards the window. It hovered uncertainly by the window for a second and then suddenly made a dash for freedom like bath water down a plug hole. Sue tried to arrest it by grabbing a large red lever marked '**ON**' ....

"I say! You in there – kindly open up!"

Jim came to lying on the floor. He was conscious of more banging at the door, only this time it was accompanied by a querulous, aristocratic voice.

Sue helped Jim to his feet.

"Get up Jim – there's been a little mistake!"

Jim looked round. The room was different with no windows and the panoramic view was of a small town.

"Where on earth are we now?"

"Don't panic! We seem to be in a place called Malvern – in .. er .. August 1853 – let's have a look at your Wikipedia"

She furrowed her brow, stared into space and quoted.

"The health-giving properties of Malvern water and the natural beauty of the surroundings led to the development of Malvern from 1842 as a world-famous spa with resources for invalids and tourists, seeking cures, rest and entertainment."

Meanwhile, Simon was angrily tugging at the door.

"Look Jim," said Sue briskly.

"We're a little way off your timeline

now and only Simon has the
resources to get you back home.
He's a selfish pig but if we help
him with his mission he'll
probably help you."
Before Jim could ask what
Simon's mission was, a portly old
man staggered through the now
open door holding a hip flask.
"I'm sorry doctor!" he said to
Simon
"I hadn't realised you were in there
with patients. I only missed one
drink at St Ann's Well and now
they're after me and I need
somewhere to hide this!"
He hastily pushed the hip flask
into Sue's pocket.
Simon, assuming an authoritative
air twirled his stethoscope

nonchalantly.

"We're finished in here Sir. May I ask how you feel today?"

"Cold, wet and hungry! I'd kill for a good steak and beer and a decent cigar. It's sheer torture down there in Tudor House. Let me tell you about the terrible descending douche ......"

But Simon interrupted him with further questions.

Sue turned to Jim.

"He's trying to find out whether the man's a philosophical zombie.", she muttered.

"A WHAT?", exclaimed Jim.

"A philosophical zombie", repeated Sue, "or p-zombie as we say in the EPU. P-zombies are supposed to be the same as real people, only not conscious but I've never met one. Ontology were experimenting to see if it was real and then Epistemology wanted to know what it knew but somehow it escaped on the way. Simon's just heard that it came here through the Edinburgh Obscura a few days before we did. His mission is to find it quick before it does something silly like coming across a really critical uncertainty and creating a rogue timeline. Hey – look at the man's shoe!"

Pushing Simon aside she trod heavily on the man's foot. He let out an ear-splitting yell and attracted the attention of two muscular attendants in white coats.

"There he is!" said one grabbing the man's arms.

"Come along now Sir! You've only seven more wells to visit this morning and then you're down again for the douche before lunch."

"Noooo – not the douche! Please not the douche again. Not the douche ...."

They whisked him off.

"Why did you do that Sue?", raged Simon, 'I was sounding him out so subtly and now you've ruined it!

"Oh no I've not!" countered Sue triumphantly.

"His clothes and shoes were soaking wet yet he wasn't conscious of that. He's definitely your p-zombie even though he cunningly pretends to feel pain. Now maybe we can get Jim home?"

"Sue, he's wearing a cold compress!" Simon sighed, exasperated, "They all do here – it's called a 'Neptune Girdle'. It's all part of the spa's famous water cure!"

Sue's reply was inaudible.

Jim pushed the door wide open and was surprised to find it led directly to the outside and onto a path descending a steep hillside dotted with bushes and small trees. They all made their way slowly downhill passing several groups of patients wielding long walking sticks. Simon insisted on engaging many patients in conversation and at last they reached St Ann's Well. The area outside the well house was populated by visitors, several on the donkeys used to convey the less mobile up the slope from the town below.

St Ann's Well, Malvern (By Jim Linwood, CC BY 2.0 via Wikimedia Commons)

Simon confronted a pale but severe-looking lady resting on a bench with an anxious footman in attendance.

"May I ask how you feel today Madam?"

She regarded Simon icily.

"I will request you not to address me, Sir."

The footman stood up and moved menacingly between her and Simon. Simon bowed.

"My apologies, Madam. Dr Fitzroy-Davidson from Edinburgh at your service. We were in fact introduced the other day.", he lied, "Now let me see your tongue!"

Surprisingly, the lady obeyed. Simon examined her tongue gravely, slowly gyrating his stethoscope in front of her face. "He's showing off again!" said Sue to Jim.

Sue, anxious to improve her knowledge of the water cure, took the footman aside and told him that she and her brother had just arrived and what could he tell her about things here? He was happy to oblige.

"I've only been here a few days myself but I've seen plenty! I'm told it costs 5 guineas for a week in Tudor House. You're up at 5 am, then stripped and wrapped in a wet sheet. An hour later you sit naked in a bath while they pour a pitcher of cold water over you. After dressing, you set off with the others up the hillside, drinking

water at every single well and after
all that there's only bread, butter,
treacle and milk for breakfast –
not forgetting water! After
breakfast you see the doctor for
your bath orders. Worst of all is
the terrible douche bath in the
garden but I'll spare your tender
ears the details Miss."
But Sue urged him on.
"A hogshead of icy water falls on
naked you from a huge pipe 20
feet above – and for the best part
of two minutes! I tell you, It's like
a thunderstorm – you should hear
'em scream and yell! Some get
knocked right over. A man was
even hit by an icicle and hurt his
back!"
Sue asked him how his lady could

possibly withstand such treatment. He glanced at the lady sorrowfully.

"She's not well enough for the douche yet and between you and me, she never will be. Her father visited yesterday and told me there's no hope at all for her now but she believes in the water cure all the same – great pity after all she did nursing our boys in the Crimea. Oh! Excuse me – Florence wants another glass of water!"

"Don't you worry!", said Sue quickly, who was moved by the footman's story.

"You stay here with her. Give me her flask and I'll bring the water back from the well."

When Sue returned with the

flask Simon had taken leave of the lady and was now talking to an attendant. Sue gave the flask to the footman.

"Thank you kindly. Miss Nightingale will be grateful." Astonished, Sue bowed politely to the famous nurse. As they moved away she told Jim not to tell Simon who the lady was so Jim stayed silent while Simon, having dismissed the attendant, informed them that the lady was definitely not a p-zombie.

"In fact, she has brucellosis and is terminally ill." he announced pompously.

"I give her 2 weeks at the most. But more importantly, she says there's some very strange goings-on in Tudor House – something about a 'Bridge of Sighs'. Sounds like p-zombie activity to me so I've made arrangements to get us in there. Follow me!" He strode on purposefully towards the town followed by Jim and Sue who lingered some distance behind.

Now Jim happened to know that Florence Nightingale lived to be 90 and put this to Sue. She was smiling.

"Simon thinks we're on a timeline where Florence dies prematurely and the nursing profession is set back by decades – but little does he know.", she chuckled.

This was all beyond Jim but by now they had entered the town and reached the imposing new building that was Tudor House. It started to rain heavily and Simon beckoned them to hurry. He knocked loudly on the door and it was opened by the same attendant he had talked with on the hillside. "We've been expecting you Dr Fitzroy-Davidson. Do come in Sir – let me take your wet coat. Please follow me with your patients." They followed him up several flights of stairs and finally into a short corridor guarded by an attendant at each end. "You do know that Dr Gully imposes strict segregation? The bridge we're on now connects Tudor House for gentlemen with the ladies' accommodation in Holyrood House."

He pointed to the heavy door at the Holyrood end of the corridor. "Needless to say only staff are allowed to use this bridge. The guards never let a patient pass unaccompanied by staff – some gentlemen call it the 'Bridge of Sighs'! The lady will be accommodated in Holyrood House of course and her brother in Tudor House."

Jim and Sue exchanged puzzled glances.

"If you would be kind enough to wait here Dr Fitzroy-Davidson with your er .. patients I will summon attendants to escort them to their rooms.."

He carefully spread out Simon's damp coat on a chair and left.

Holyrood House, the Bridge of Sighs and Tudor House in 2015

Simon explained that he'd registered Jim and Sue for a week's water cure at Tudor House, this being an excellent opportunity to investigate the strange goings-on.

"I told everyone that you're both quite mad and given to impersonation. Whatever you do will always be above suspicion! Clever eh?"

This was not well received and Sue protested loudly. Just then, the same two muscular attendants, who earlier had dealt with the old man, entered the corridor. Having been instructed to humour lunatics before attempting restraint, the duo paused deferentially, straitjackets at the ready.

"We'll take over now, Dr Fitzroy-Davidson" said one to Jim after a few moments.

"Now come along James", said the other to Simon. "We'll have a nice glass of water and then into the garden to join the douche queue – you'll feel a lot better after a good shower Sir."

Simon blinked. "I'm Dr Fitzroy-Davidson you numbskull!"

"Of course you are Sir and a good doctor too, with a real stethoscope but it's time for a nice glass of water. Come along now Sir!" and the attendant grabbed Simon's arm.

While Sue and Simon had been arguing, Jim, not short of initiative when under pressure, had sidled over to the chair where Simon's damp white coat had been left and had put it on. Now he approached the astonished Simon and snatched the stethoscope from his neck.

"Come along now doctor.", commanded Jim, "You can have it back later – you don't want to miss the douche do you?."

"You can't do this to me!", Simon spluttered.

"Look Jim, this is the wrong timeline for you and you'll never get home without me. Now send for the other attendant and we'll sort it all out!"

Sue was not slow to put him right.

"I'll have you know we **are** on

Jim's timeline. The robovirus I added to Florence Nightingale's water is making short work of her brucellosis. She'll live to be 90 just like Jim's 2014 Wikipedia says."

Simon was aghast.

"You know very well reality should be left to take its course. You don't alter timelines for your own convenience! If the lady really is Florence Nightingale her survival or not is a critical uncertainty for nursing. You've significantly altered the future of nursing and probably the future of all sorts of related things on this – this rogue timeline!"

"Bah! – its a better timeline anyway!", retorted Sue.

"It's quite contrary to EPU policy

and if this really is a rogue timeline you're in **big** trouble."
The two attendants, amused at first by these apparently insane ramblings, finally ran out of patience. Deftly securing Simon in one of the straitjackets they marched him away protesting loudly.
"Don't worry about the lady", Jim shouted after them. "I have to take her to see Dr Gully."
The attendants waved in acquiescence and whisked Simon off to enjoy a week's water cure.

When Simon's shouts were barely audible, Jim and Sue strode down the corridor passing the guard who waved them on after a nominal glance at

Jim's white coat. They proceeded down the Tudor House stairs at a brisk pace.

"Hey there!", somebody called.

It was the footman.

"How's Miss Nightingale?", asked Sue politely.

"Very well indeed thanks to your robovirus. She's recovering well – even working on her Crimean report."

Sue was flabbergasted.

"Don't look so stunned!" laughed the footman.

"I came through the Edinburgh Obscura only a few days before you. Fortunately Florence was looking out for a new footman and I like the job so much I'm definitely not going back to the

EPU."

Sue stared at him in amazement. "You're the p-zombie they're all looking for", she squealed.

"Well yes I am and just as conscious as you are, honest! I was at my wit's end with worry about poor Florence when I saw you last. I don't have the resources to get her decent medication but I do analyse everything she drinks. When I saw the robovirus I figured out you were from the EPU, probably sent to take me back, so I kept quiet but now she's as bright as a lark and I can't thank you enough!"

"Glad to help!", said Sue, "But I'm in real trouble if the EPU finds out I've created a rogue timeline."

"Don't worry!", replied the p-zombie. "They always think that p-zombies barge around infospace creating rogue timelines. You can truthfully say that I gave Florence the drink with the robovirus. What's more, you'll get the credit for identifying a dangerous p-zombie and they won't bother me now on a rogue timeline. My only wish is to stay with Florence and serve her as long as I possibly can."

Jim thought this was pretty noble for an unconscious zombie but was anxious to get out of Tudor House. They wished the p-zombie the best of luck and quickly escaped.

As they headed for the Obscura

room Sue stopped several times to refresh herself from the flask the old man had given her and she was in high spirits as they made their way up the hillside.

"Simon should be out of the way for a bit so now.", she chortled gleefully, "So now's the time to get you to your 2104."

"2014!" interjected Jim.

"Sorry, but you know how I am with numbers!", said Sue with sincerity and then remarked on the high quality of Malvern water. She offered Jim a swig from the hip flask, now nearly empty.

Taking a hearty swig he nearly choked.

"That's not water!", he spluttered. "It's port! The old guy didn't want it to be found on him!"

"Don't you believe it!", exclaimed Sue enthusiastically. "Malvern water really is this good – little wonder all these famous people come for the cure. I've never felt more alive!"

Fortunately no one was in the Obscura room when they arrived as Sue could not wait to demonstrate her expertise.

"No fancy control panel for me Jim! Look – no hands! Now It was 2410 you wanted? Just joking! 2014 it is and space co-ordinates for your bench in Edinburgh – no problem at all!"

"Yeah!, 2014, 2014, 2014, ..." repeated Jim hopefully.

"Cut and paste is always tricky as you know but infospace – anything can happen that the laws of physics allow and of course infospace projection is naturally probabilistic in time and space but with a combination of EPU resources and my expertise, we **will** triumph. We don't want to project you into the middle of the sun! – ha! ha!"

Jim was not amused and wished she would get on with whatever she did but Sue continued to explain.

"You'll lose all memory of being here and simply think you've been asleep for about 20 minutes. I'm setting the projector for your timeline at 2104 – I mean 2014. All systems green and go!", she shouted excitedly and closed her eyes. Jim held his breath.

Jim woke with a start. Glancing at his watch, he'd been asleep on the bench for about 20 minutes. Everything around him seemed normal and he was glad that Sue had succeeded in sending him home although he did remember everything. There was a man sitting beside him, apparently just waking up. Jim stood up, stretched for a moment and went on his way – so did the man. Jim turned round and confronted his identical twin......

Jim woke with a start. Glancing at his watch, he'd been asleep on the bench for about 20 minutes. There was a man sitting beside him, apparently just waking up. The man stood up, stretched for a moment and went on his way. So did Jim – the man turned round and Jim confronted his identical twin....

Jim woke with a start. Glancing at his watch, he'd been asleep on the bench for about 20 minutes. Sue was sitting beside him.

"Excuse me, have you the time?", she said politely.

"What's going on Sue?", asked Jim. Sue frowned.

"You should have lost your memory but the good news is that cut and paste really isn't necessary because you're here already if you see what I mean." Jim did not see and began to look around as the courtyard darkened. Sue frowned.

"Hmm... I see no more Jims around here so the space co-ordinates must be wrong", she announced, "but the time doesn't seem right either. You did say 2140 didn't you Jim?"

Jim cast his eyes heavenwards as a gigantic flying saucer hovered above them.

"Don't panic!" whimpered Sue.

Jim woke with a start. Glancing at his watch, he'd been asleep on the bench for about 20 minutes but now he was wearing a damp white coat and a stethoscope hung round his neck. A young lady in fancy dress was watching him intently from the other side of the courtyard.

"Effing medical student stunt!", he muttered to himself remembering it was rag week. He took off the coat wondering how they'd put it on him, stuffed the stethoscope into the pocket and left everything on the bench. He stood up, stretched for a moment and went on his way....

Jim woke with a start. Glancing at his watch, he'd been asleep on the bench for about 20 minutes. He stood up, stretched for a moment and went on his way....

Jim woke with a start...

THE GREAT MALVERN PARADOX

ABOUT THE AUTHOR

Gordon Lockhart is an academic author who taught and researched in electronics and communications engineering for many years. On retiring, he continued his interest in education by running an education website and blogging about Massive Open Online Courses (MOOCs). After participating in a MOOC on introductory philosophy he was inspired to write several science fiction short stories illustrating some philosophical dilemmas in a light-hearted way.

Printed in Great Britain
by Amazon

83510585R00068